SPARTACUS

THE SPIDER

Published in 2010 by Creative Editions
P.O. Box 227, Mankato, MN 56002 USA
www.thecreativecompany.us
Creative Editions is an imprint of The Creative Company.
Designed by Rita Marshall. Edited by Aaron Frisch

Printed by Corporate Graphics in the United States of America.

Library of Congress Cataloging-in-Publication Data
Delessert, Etienne.
Spartacus the spider / written and illustrated by Etienne Delessert.
Summary: Spartacus is a little spider who struggles to spin strong strands,
but with determination and some encouragement he succeeds in making
the strongest string ever, then worries about its repercussions.
ISBN 978-1-56846-213-4
[1. Spider webs—Fiction. 2. Spiders—Fiction.
3. Determination (Personality trait)—Fiction.
4. Environmental protection—Fiction.] I. Title.
PZ7.D3832Sp 2010 [E]– dc22 2010004176

CPSIA: 012910 PO1182

First edition
2 4 6 8 9 7 5 3 1

ETIENNE DELESSERT

SPARTACUS

THE SPIDER

CREATIVE EDITIONS

Honor and fame!
This is what my
parents wished for
me. So they named
me Spartacus.

I grew up in the sky, an acrobat on high wires.

I learned to spin threads,
but I was not very good at it.
Threads broke. Webs drooped.
I became overwhelmed by a
deep sense of failure.

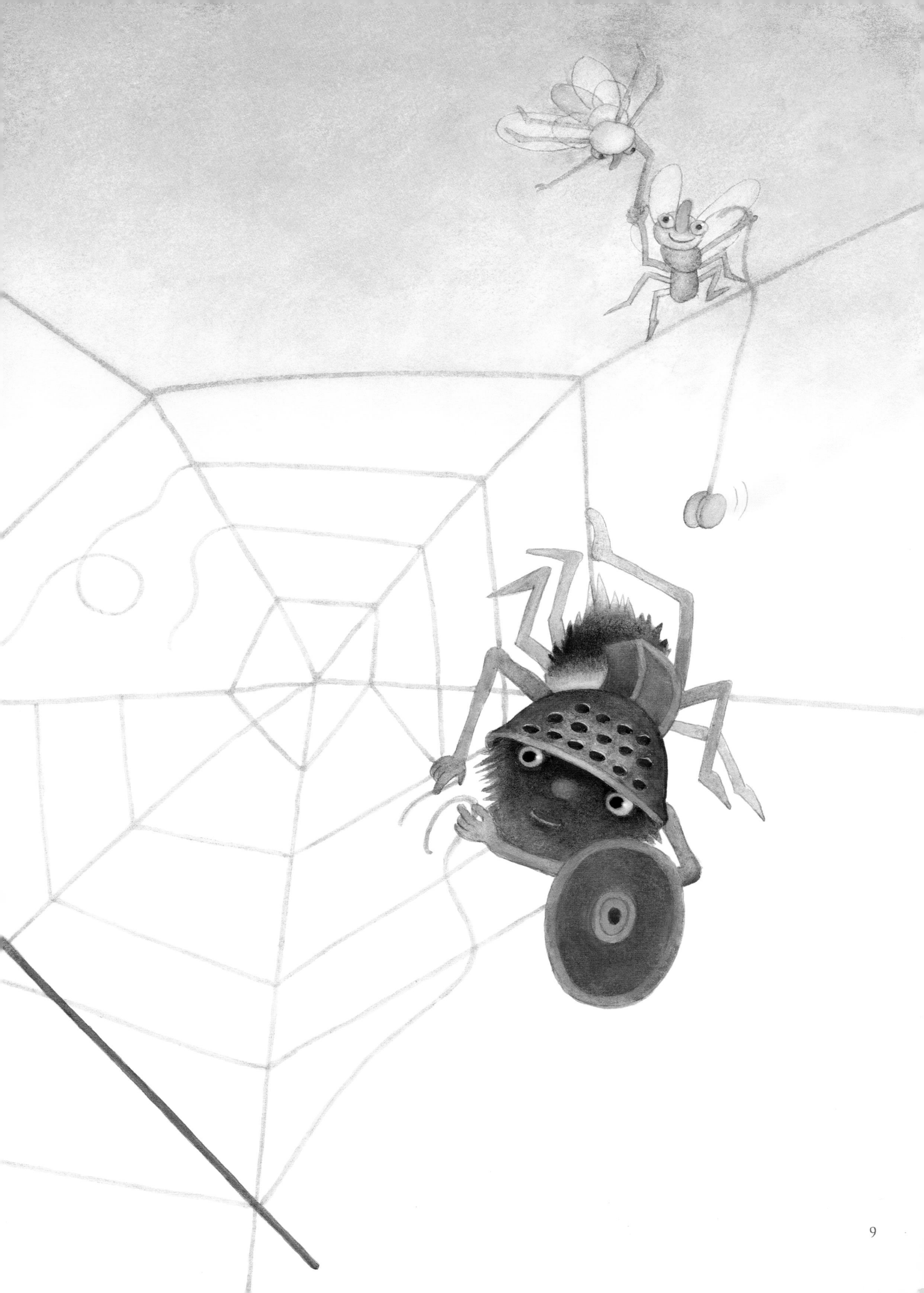

Flies laughed at me.

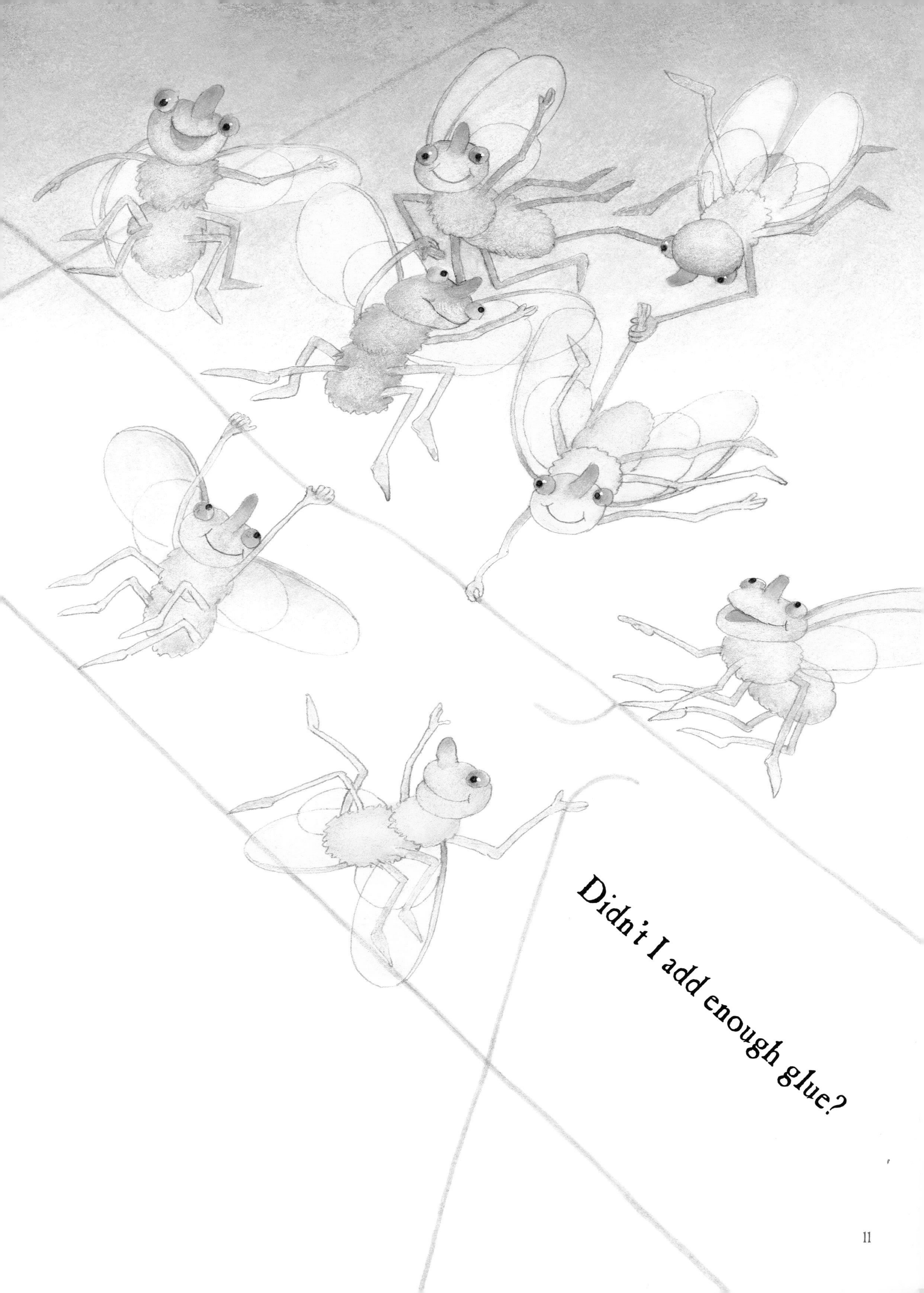

Didn't I add enough glue?

Moths flew right through
my net! I was humiliated.
And hungry, too.

I needed to seriously improve
the quality of my silk.

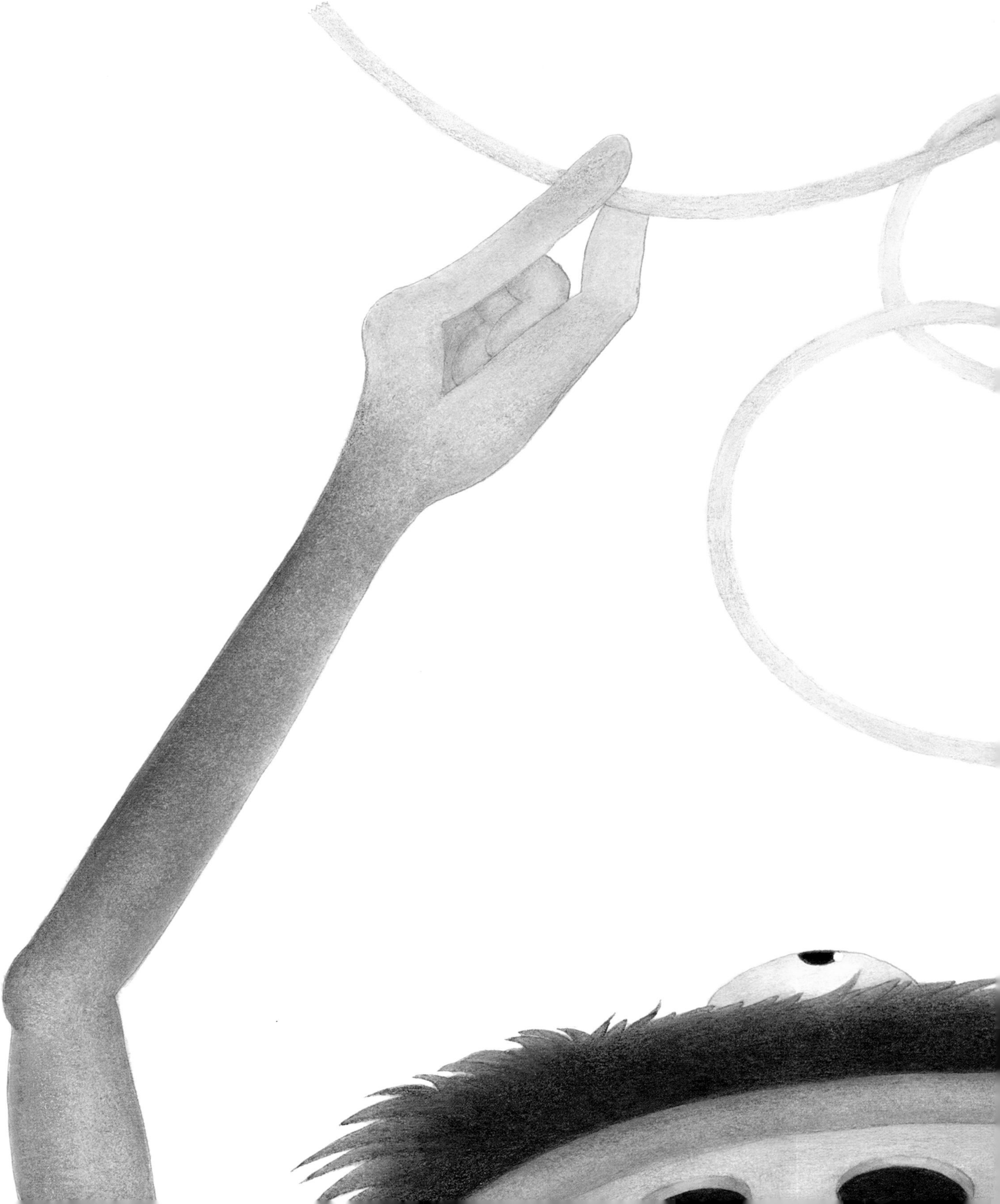

I closed my eyes.
As I inhaled the
scents of the forest,
a mouse passed by
and whispered to me
some very odd news.

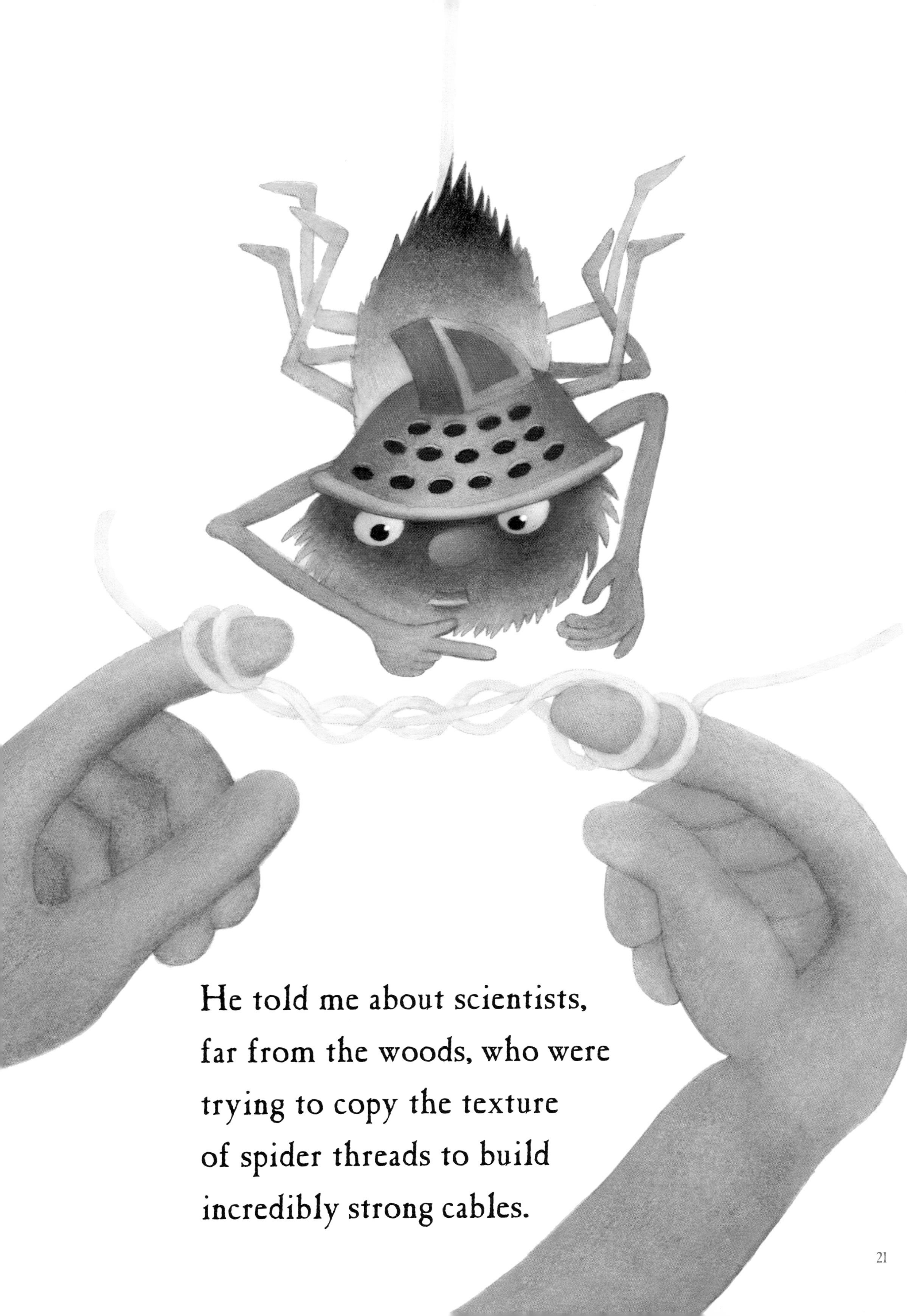

He told me about scientists,
far from the woods, who were
trying to copy the texture
of spider threads to build
incredibly strong cables.

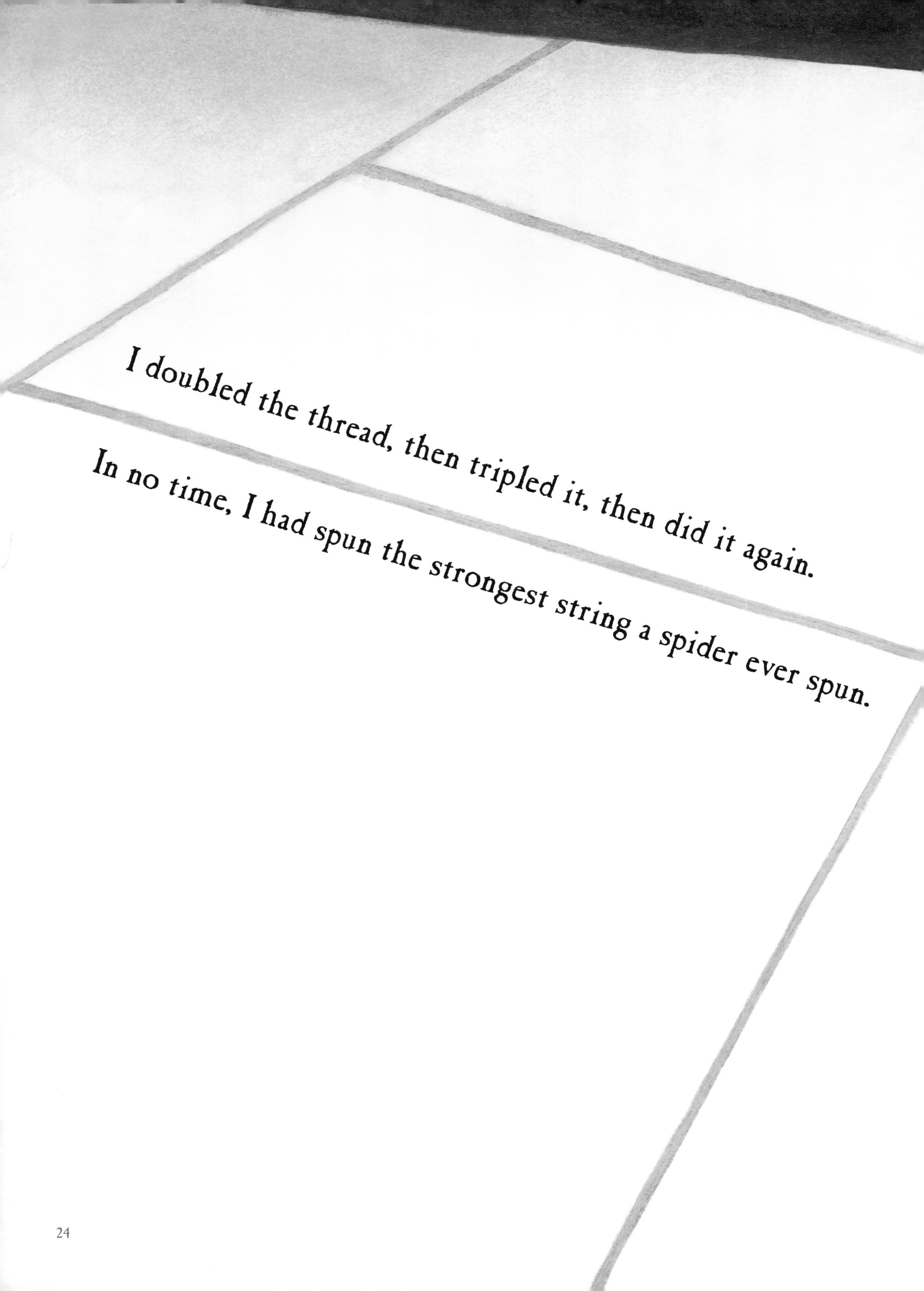

I doubled the thread, then tripled it, then did it again.

In no time, I had spun the strongest string a spider ever spun.

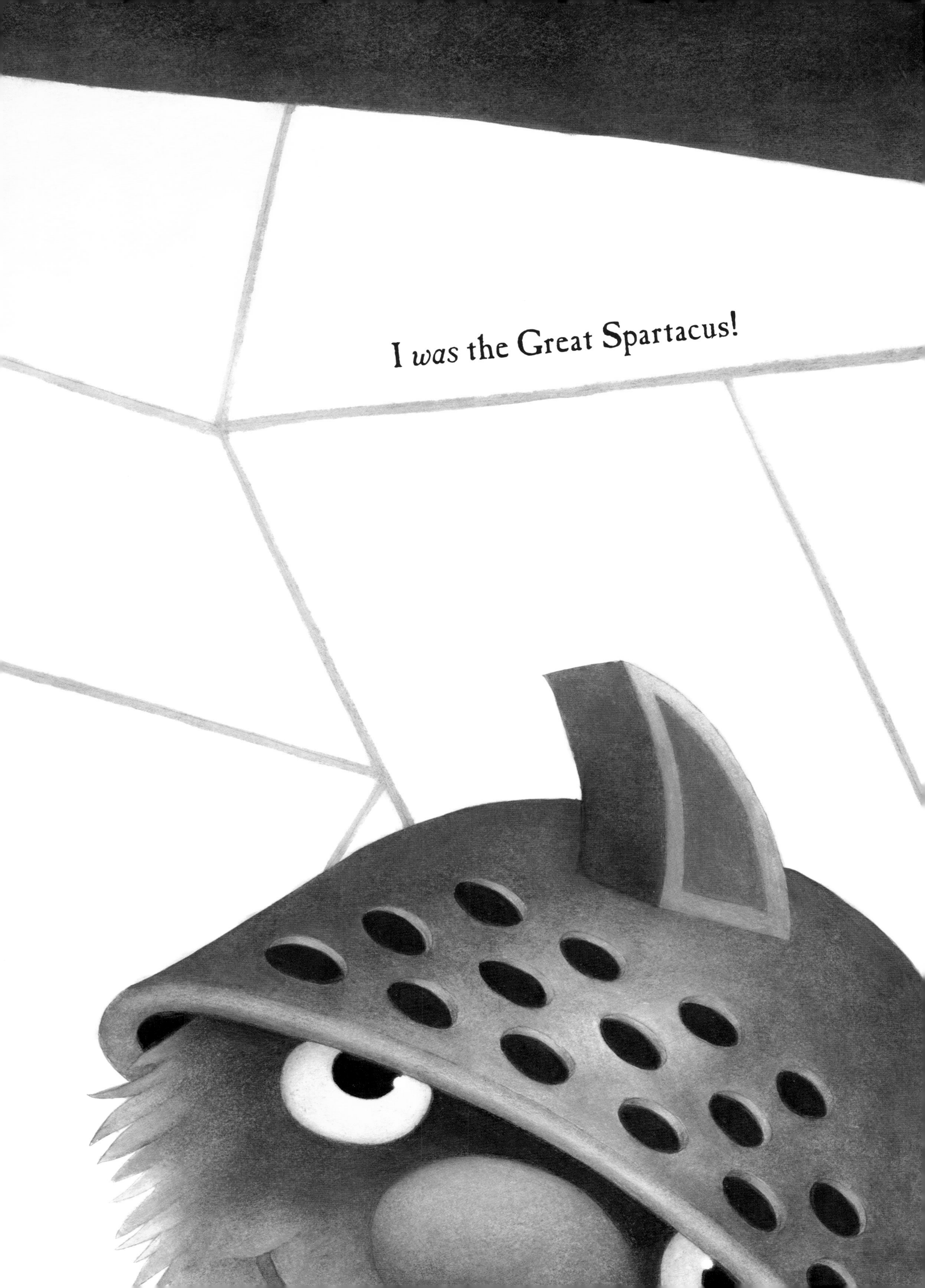

I *was* the Great Spartacus!

A huge moth stuck to the thread,
then two humbled flies. I cheered.

But then I worried.

If my web couldn't ever be
broken, the world's entire moth
population might pile up in it...
And flies, even birds!
Airplanes?

I shivered. The world would become

a giant, terrifying net. Unbreakable for eternity.

So I went back to spinning
my old, loppy threads.

Flies flew, and moths broke through. I didn't mind being me.

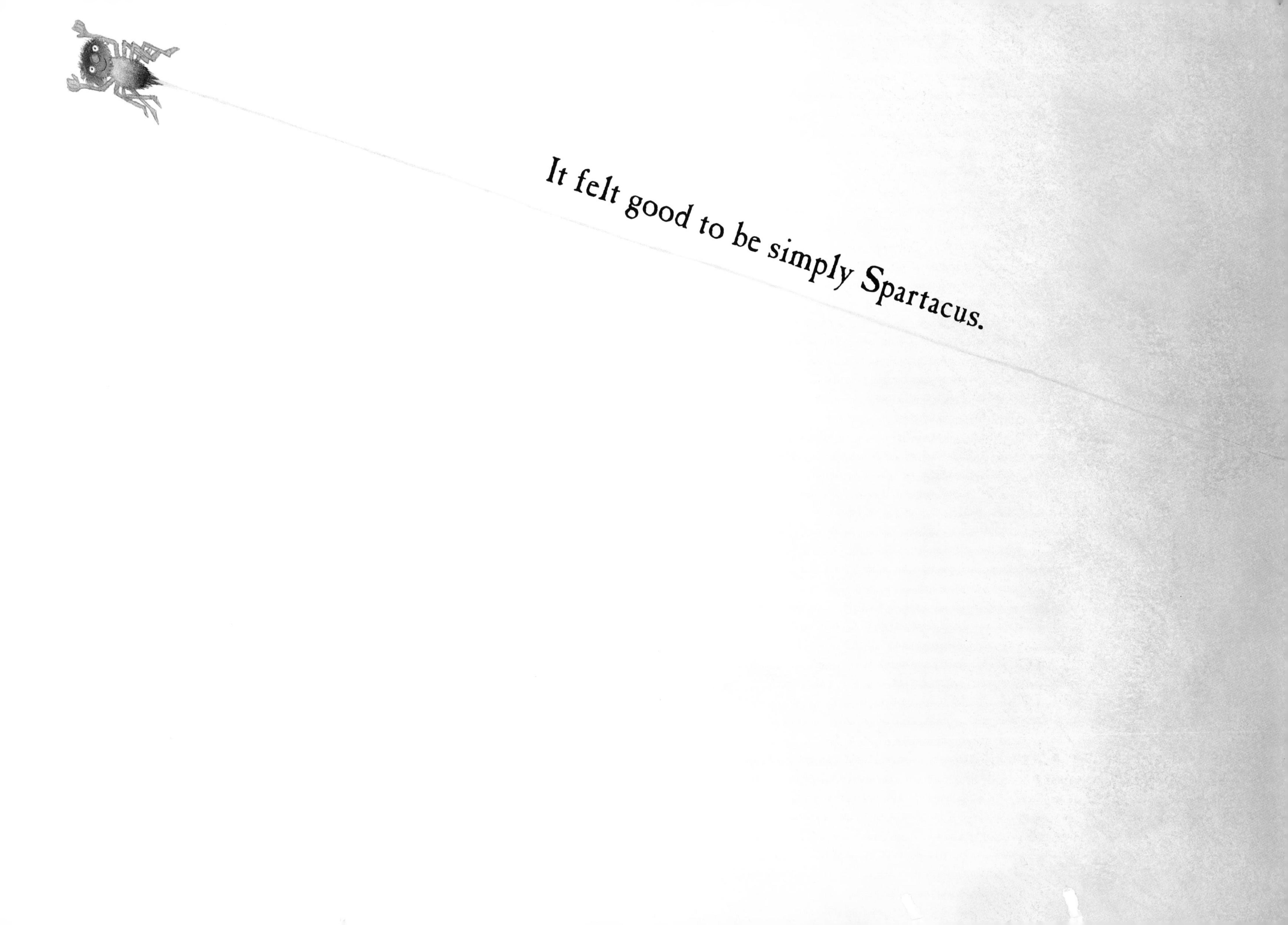

It felt good to be simply Spartacus.